'Everyone can get involved in building the *SS Henry*.
It could spark raids on other dads' toolsheds.
Recommended.'

Magpies

'... a joyful, read-aloud text that celebrates the power of a child's imagination.'

Take 5

'A wonderful picture book about the power of play and its role in enhancing
the imagination. And the pictures of the beach and the sea are so beautiful—I loved this one.
Highly recommended for 5-8 year olds.'

SAETA Newsletter

'Ross Mueller finds poetry in the tools needed to put the boat together:
hammer, saw, drill and drop sheet. Craig Smith's detailed, character-driven
illustrations, composed with film-like angles and perspectives, make the
project look easy and fun.'

Weekend Australian

'Mueller has captured the mood of this young boy beautifully, showing his
curious and creative mind. The illustrations are delightful.'

Reading Time

For Henry and Stan

For the children who love to build boats and for the grown-ups who love to help them

—RM

For Barnacle Bee Buoy

—CS

The Boy Who Built the Boat

Ross Mueller ⚒ Craig Smith

ALLEN&UNWIN

Down at the bottom of Henry's backyard
is a shed where his dad builds boats.
It is filled with tools that hang on the walls
and sawdust and big ideas.

There are hammers and nails
and drills and saws and useful things
that his dad likes to keep there, because,

"You never know
when you might need them."

Early one day,
when his dad was working in the shed
Henry decided it was time he built
a boat of his own.
So...

Henry set out to build
a boat that day
and he took along a hammer
to hammer in all the nails.

And you never
know when
you might need
a hammer.

Henry went out to
build a boat that day
and he took along
a drill,
to drill some holes
in the wood...

and you never know
when you might need
a drill or a hammer
or a drill...or a hammer.

Henry went out to build a boat that day
and he took along a saw, to cut a mast for the boat...

and you never know
   when you might need a saw
      or a drill
         or a hammer or a saw or a drill...
         or a hammer.

Henry went out to build a boat that day
and he took along a drop sheet,
to use for the sails on his boat...

and you never know
when you might need a drop sheet
or a saw or a drill or a hammer
or a drop sheet or a hammer or a drill
or a saw or a drop sheet or a drill...
or a hammer.

Henry went out to build a boat that day
and he took along his sister to make sure
he measured everything correctly.

And you never know when you might need
a sister with a Teddy or a saw or a drill
or a hammer or a Teddy with a drill
or a sister with a saw or a drill
or a drop sheet
or a hammer with a sister
or a Teddy or a saw…
or a hammer.

Henry went out to build a boat that day
and he took along his wheelbarrow
to see if the boat would float.

He filled the wheelbarrow
with water from the hose
and soon it became his ocean.

He held up the boat for his dad to see,
and he said very loudly
in his best Captain's voice,

"Good luck to the SS Henry!"

The boat bobbled and it wobbled
and it tumbled and it tacked
and the wind was behind it
and the ocean was rough.
The mast was straight
and the sail was filled
and it all held together

and the SS Henry was strong.

His sister was excited
and his dad was impressed.
He had used all the tools
from the shed down the back,
the hammer and the drill
and the saw and the drop sheet,
the useful bits and pieces
that were needed that day.

Henry had put them all together
and created something special.
He had built...

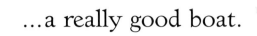

...a really good boat.

With special thanks to Jodie and Erica and Hilary
and the A&U Crew aboard the SS Henry. —RM

This paperback edition published in 2009

First published in 2006

Allen & Unwin
83 Alexander St
Crows Nest NSW 2065
Australia
Phone: (61 2) 8425 0100
Fax: (61 2) 9906 2218
Email: info@allenandunwin.com
Web: www.allenandunwin.com

National Library of Australia Cataloguing-in-Publication entry:
Mueller, Ross, 1967– .
The boy who built the boat.
For young children.
Illustrated by Craig Smith.
ISBN: 978 174175 588 6 (pbk.)
A823.4

Designed by Andrew Cunningham – Studio Pazzo
Typeset in Hadriano
Printed in China at Everbest Printing Co

1 3 5 7 9 10 8 6 4 2

The illustrations were drawn with a nibbed pen,
and coloured using gouache ink and paint.
www.craigsmithillustration.com

Ross Mueller

I wrote this story for my son Henry. We used to sing it together before bedtime.
The list of the tools in the story is what we would collect in our song before sleep.
Originally it was about building a fence, because that's what he wanted to do. Construction,
construction, construction! At the time, a fence seemed like a good idea. It was tall and very
impressive when it was finished. But a fence keeps somebody or something out. The ocean has
no fences and our imaginations are free to bob about in the waves, and so our fence
became a boat. I love this book and I love Craig's illustrations.
They remind me of a very happy boy.

Craig Smith

This enterprising little fellow, Henry, is so like me as a boy. I wonder how Ross,
the author, knew this? I learnt my skills of bush carpentry by mucking around in the
shed, with tools that didn't need powercords. You're never too young to learn.
Unfortunately my father was not skilled with woodworking tools, but fortunately he was skilled
at drawing. My own son is far more skilled with woodworking tools than I am, and
I can't remember teaching him anything! Except for a love of making things.
The illustrations were done in a deliberately wet washy way,
suitable for boats and puddles.